Plush and Tatty on the Beach

by
Molly Brett

© THE MEDICI SOCIETY LTD · LONDON 1987.   Printed in England.   B92.   ISBN 0 85503 092 5

Plush the big teddy bear had overslept so that, when his little friend Tatty came running in with a letter, he woke up with such a start that he fell out of bed and landed BUMP on the floor.

'Oh Plush!' squeaked Tatty, 'I have just had this letter from Aunt Pushy Bear. She wants us to stay with her in a caravan by the sea, and she will fetch us tomorrow.'

Plush sat on the floor and read the letter. 'You don't look very pleased,' he remarked looking at Tatty. 'Oh Plush,' squeaked his friend, 'it is very kind of Aunt Pushy Bear, but she does have so many IDEAS, and everyone is always pushed in to help with them!'

'Trust me,' growled Plush, 'nobody is going to push *me* and we'll have fun at the seaside with your aunt.'

The next morning Plush and Tatty were ready with their luggage, waiting for Aunt Pushy Bear to collect them in her car. It was a very small car and Aunt Pushy Bear was a busy little bear with a fluffy fur coat and a large pair of sun-glasses. 'All ready for the beach, dears?' she enquired. 'Tatty shall sit in front and your friend must go in the back with the luggage.'

Plush squeezed into the back seat and the luggage was piled on top of him. 'Off we go,' squealed Aunt Pushy Bear starting the car. But – something strange was happening – the back part sank down under the weight of Plush and all the luggage, while the front wheels rose in the air and as Aunt Pushy Bear looked round she nearly drove into a wall. So the luggage had to be moved to the front seat on top of Tatty and away they went.

It was not far to the sea and
the caravan. When they arrived
Aunt Pushy Bear said to Tatty and Plush, 'We are having a
barbecue tonight and the Grizzlies are coming, such nice
bears, and you can play with the children, but first we must
catch some fish,' and she bustled the two bears off with
fishing lines.

Presently Tatty squeaked, 'I've got a bite!' but the fish pulled
so hard and the rock she was on was so slippery, that she and
Plush ended up in the water.

Tatty scrambled out with a big fish while Plush was still
splashing about. 'Something has got hold of my foot', he
growled. So Tatty and her aunt pulled him out with a large
lobster clinging to his toe. 'Too big to cook it for the barbecue,'
sighed Aunt Pushy Bear as it fell back into the sea. 'It was an
Enormous lobster,' boasted Plush, 'and *I* caught it all by myself.'
But Tatty squeaked, '*We* thought the lobster caught *you*, Plush!'.

Aunt Pushy Bear put the fish on the barbecue to cook and the Grizzly family arrived. Both the little bears were grizzling and Plush was told to take them for a walk.

'And be sure they do not fall off the cliff or tumble into the sea!' ordered Aunt Pushy Bear.

Meanwhile Tatty helped with the barbecue and when it was ready Plush was called. 'But *where* are our children?' growled the Grizzlies when he appeared. 'In a lobster pot,' exclaimed Plush looking pleased with himself, 'you *said* not to let them tumble off the cliff or fall into the sea, so they are quite safe in there.'

When the little Grizzlies had been released from the lobster pot, grizzling louder than ever, all was ready for the barbecue to begin. Just then down swooped a crowd of seagulls all snatching at the fish but, after much growling, squeaking and waving of paws, they flew away and the teddy bears were able to enjoy their supper after all.

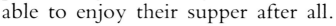
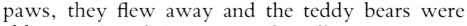
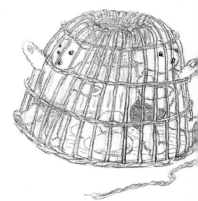

At bedtime there was no room for Plush in the little caravan so he had to sleep in a tent beside it. But during the night the wind started to blow and it blew the tent down on top of him. Poor Plush now had no shelter at all, so, with some difficulty, he wriggled under the caravan and was soon fast asleep.

Presently Tatty was awakened by a strange sound, 'ZZZzzzzz!' Then Aunt Pushy Bear woke up too and they listened... 'Something is *under* the caravan!' she whispered and, hopping out, peered underneath it. In the moonlight she spied a large pair of furry feet – they belonged to Plush and he was SNORING! So both little bears went back to bed and were soon fast asleep again.

In the morning after breakfast Aunt Pushy Bear said they would play with her beach ball, but Plush kicked it so hard that it landed BUMP right in the middle of the Grizzly Bears' picnic.

This was terrible and Aunt Pushy Bear hastened to tell them how sorry she was and sent Plush and Tatty to a little baker's shop nearby to buy a delicious honey cake with nuts on top for their picnic. So, instead of grizzling, the bears invited the three to join the party, and Aunt Pushy Bear announced she had a wonderful idea. 'We will have sports on the beach tomorrow,' and everyone agreed it was a splendid plan.

Aunt Pushy Bear settled down for a little nap while Plush and Tatty enjoyed the ice-creams she had given them. Then they built a fine sand castle, and afterwards went off to explore some rock pools where Plush caught Tatty in his net instead of a shrimp.

Later they returned to wake up Aunt Pushy Bear asleep on the beach... but Aunt Pushy Bear wasn't there! The tide had come in and she had had to scramble up the cliff away from the water, and there Plush and Tatty found her – stuck half-way. She could not go up and she could not go down.

Big Ben Bear, the boatman, was called. He lowered a rope and Aunt Pushy Bear tied it around herself. Then Big Ben, Plush and Tatty pulled, and tugged, and heaved, and up over the cliff edge came Aunt Pushy Bear.

'What an adventure!' she giggled, 'but where are my sun-glasses?'

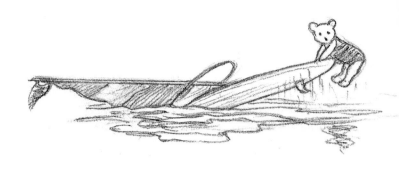

Big Ben now kindly offered to lend them his windsurfing board and Plush and Aunt Pushy Bear were soon trying to show each other how to sail it.

First Aunt Pushy Bear fell overboard, then Plush lost his balance and went into the sea with a big SPLASH, and poor Tatty was left drifting away from the shore alone on the surfboard.

So Big Ben had to rescue them in his boat. He was rather cross and hung those three wet teddy bears over his washing line. 'That will keep you out of mischief, and you will soon drip-dry there,' he chuckled.

Early next morning Aunt Pushy Bear was bustling about very busily indeed. Plush and Tatty were ordered to go along the beach carrying notice boards to announce the sports, while the Grizzly Bear family helped with the flags, posts, sacks and ropes, borrowed from Big Ben at whose cottage they were staying. He kept all these things in his shed, all ready for the summer sailing races, along with fishing nets and a smell of tar.

Soon big and little bears were gathering on the beach ready for the sports to begin, and off they went in the sack race with Plush easily coming first.

However, Aunt Pushy Bear soon discovered that *his* sack had holes in it for his feet. 'No prize for *you!*,' she snapped. What fun all the teddy bears had – tumbling over each other in the three-legged race, getting all tangled up in the skipping race, and Plush falling head–over–heels in the high jump. It was sad that Tatty did *not* win the egg-and-spoon race because she had used the sticky spoon from a pot of honey.

The sports ended with a tug-of-war and, when the rope broke, all the teddy bears fell on top of one another. 'A dead heat,' announced Aunt Pushy Bear and everyone clapped both teams as winners.

Then there was dancing by the light of the moon with Plush and Tatty playing on their fiddles.

Aunt Pushy Bear was a little upset when she saw that Big Ben the boatman was wearing *her* sun-glasses which he had found on the beach, but as he had been so kind she gladly agreed that he should keep them. 'They do suit him and perhaps *I* look better without glasses,' she giggled.

To complete the event Aunt Pushy Bear presented the prizes and Tatty presented her with a bouquet of sea holly and seaweed. At last the tide came in over the sand and the teddy bears went home to bed, all growling and squeaking what a wonderful day it had been on Teddy Bear Beach.